IMAGES OF CHRIST SERIES, VOL. 1

The Carpenter's Shop

A STORY OF BROKENNESS...AND HOPE

Kevin Hrebik

Foreword by Jeff Black

Halo ●●●●
Publishing International
www.halopublishing.com

Cover photo by Kevin Hrebik
Recreated 1st century carpenter's shop in Nazareth, Israel.
For more information, visit www.nazarethvillage.org.

For more information, contact:
Kevin Hrebik
Email Author: hopebehindbars@sbcglobal.net

ISBN 978-1-935268-30-7

Attention organizations, buyers and educational institutions: Quantity discounts are available on bulk purchases of this book for reselling, educational purposes, subscription incentives or fund raising. Please contact our Sales Department at 216-255-6756.

Halo ● ● ● ●
Publishing International
www.halopublishing.com

Printed in the United States of America

This book is dedicated to my Mom,
who helped me survive my childhood,
who has prayed for me continuously,
and who was my first best friend.

*"By a Carpenter mankind was made,
and only by that Carpenter
can mankind be remade."*

Desiderius Erasmus
(1466 – 1536)

CONTENTS

Foreword ix

Introduction xi

1. He's a Carpenter 1

2. The Master Craftsman............................ 5

3. A Walking Ghetto 9

4. The Carpenter's Shop............................ 13

5. The Carpenter's Toolbox 17

6. The Original Innocence Project........................ 23

7. *Much* More Than a Carpenter............................ 27

8. Today is the Day! 31

About the Author..................................... 35

Reviews... 37

FOREWORD

My friend Kevin knows the Carpenter and will help you know Him, too. Kevin has had what the TV show would call an "extreme makeover," which is a good thing – his structure was in rough shape.

Christian communication is filled with many testimonies, and each of them has the power to move us. People get up and testify in our church every week. Always the ones that really move me have a humble and shy quality to them, and keep the focus on the One who saves. This is Kevin's, and I bet you'll find yourself in it as well.

You're about to read a report of a wonderful remodel, and to meet the loving man who now lives inside it. And – you can enjoy the same kind of renewed home for your life, as he will show you.

Jeff Black
Pastor, St. Barnabas the Encourager
Round Rock, Texas

INTRODUCTION

What do you think God looks like? A child who once was asked this question said with wisdom beyond her years, "He looks like love." That's pretty hard to argue with, isn't it? Jesus said, *"He who has seen Me has seen the Father"* (John 14:9). The question then is what do you think Jesus looks like? Unfortunately, photography hadn't been invented yet or we might have quite a few pictures of him. The next best choice would be art or sculpture but, again, no one seems to have painted or sculpted a likeness that has survived from the first century.

What we are left with are many creative renditions through the centuries as people have tried to capture their vision of what Jesus looked like. While there is a good bit of disagreement about the Shroud of Turin, with its almost ghostly negative image of a face, what modern technology created from it was a computerized positive image, which is included here.[1] Personally, this has come to be my favorite image of Christ, even though I know it is entirely possible that this wasn't what Jesus looked like at all.

In truth, it really doesn't matter what Jesus looked like (and it seems we weren't meant to know), because scripture

---

[1] Image found at: http://romanchristendom.blogspot.com/2009/10/ave-christus-rex-viva-christo-rey-hail.html.

teaches that what is important is his nature, his attributes and his character. In fact, Ephesians 5:1 tells us to *"Be imitators of God."* In 2 Corinthians 3:18, we also discover this (emphasis added): *"And we, who with unveiled faces all reflect the Lord's glory, are being **transformed into his likeness** with ever-increasing glory, which comes from the Lord, who is the Spirit."*

Clearly, we are not being transformed into Jesus' physical likeness. On what *model* then do we base our *imitation of him* that is in progress according to the above scripture? Or to word it another way, what is our envisioned *image* of Jesus that is in process within us? Yet another way to ask the same question is what *pattern* do we use as a biblical template for our Christian lives? What *vision* of Christ do we carry within us as a guide for our transformation process? All of these questions are answered with the many images or metaphors of Christ found in scripture.

Let us look again at Jesus' words in John 14:9, *"Anyone who has seen me has seen the Father...."* Exactly what do we *see* when we "see" Jesus? We *feel* His love, we *sense* His presence, we *know* his power, we *appreciate* His attributes and *experience* some of them...but what does this composite image based on his attributes and characteristics look like in our heads? And how do we relate to it? I believe it is important to solidify our personal image of God if we intend to imitate Him.

In 1994, God inspired me to start a project, which I thought at the time was going to be a single book about the many images of Christ in scripture. Now it seems the project will become many small books instead of one large one. The Bible contains at least 100 names for God, Jesus or the Spirit, but I was looking for complete similes or metaphors (images) of Christ, including several self-proclaimed "I am..." images. I discovered a total of 19 such images: Author of Faith, Bread of Life, Bridegroom, Carpenter, Cornerstone, Door (or

Gate), Good Shepherd, Lamb of God, Light of the World, Lily of the Valley, Lion of Judah, Master Potter, Morning Star, Pearl of Great Price, Physician, Rock of Ages, Rose of Sharon, Teacher, and True Vine.

What you are holding is the first book in the series, each of which will focus on one of these beloved, timeless images. Not only that, but each will have a different purpose. *The Carpenter's Shop* focuses on my testimony and is intended to be a witnessing tool. The next book in the series, *Ten Clay Soldiers: Lessons from the Master Potter*, will focus on personal transformation, and so on.

I believe that there are no accidental passages in scripture. I believe Christ carefully and deliberately chose these precious similes and metaphors to help us *visualize* him, *relate* to him and *imitate* him. He completely embodies each of them and all of them simultaneously. Each one has: (1) *simplicity* with which anyone can readily identify, but also (2) *depth* we'll never reach and meaning we'll never exhaust, and (3) an uncanny *accuracy* we can only begin to comprehend in all its spiritual wonder and mystery.

Each image provides for us a lifetime of *following*, *understanding* and *imitating* capacity, and combined they give us all we'll ever need to learn about how to become like our Lord and to become transformed into his image. Which is your favorite? Perhaps that will change next year or in ten or twenty years. I believe our loving, all-knowing Lord not only has something for everyone in each of them but also something different at different times in our lives from the same images.

Come with me on a journey into the many fascinating, timeless and depthless images of Christ in scripture, starting with the heartwarming and easily relatable image of the Carpenter! I believe it is appropriate to start with this image because I think it is one of the easiest for people to identify with. For many, this little book might become their first personal revelation of Christ, the first image that came to life for them from the pages of a sometimes overwhelming and daunting book—the image that helped them for the very first time to understand who Jesus was, why He came to earth and, most importantly, why He surrendered His life.

Kevin Hrebik

*"He waits for us to bring him
broken things to mend."*
LeRoy Blankenship

One

He's a Carpenter

I once met a traveling evangelist and singer named LeRoy Blankenship[2] when our pastor invited him to come and lead our church in a revival. LeRoy and his wife showed up in a big bus, which was their home away from home, and his simple, country style was to play the guitar while his wife played piano and sing from the large assortment of songs he had written over the years and recorded on cassette tapes. At the time, none of them were expensive productions or big sellers because that wasn't his intent. He just sold them to congregations where he performed and, along with love offerings, it was how he and his wife made their living.

I especially remember a song of LeRoy's titled "He's a Carpenter." One line from the song remains fondly etched in my memory: *"He waits for us to bring Him broken things to mend."* What a simple and beautiful thought—we come to the Carpenter with our broken hearts, our shattered dreams

---

[2] LeRoy Blankenship Ministries: www.leroyblankenship.com. As of this writing, LeRoy has traveled the globe for 38 years, has won major music awards, including the Lifetime Achievement Award by the Christian Country Music Association and, among numerous other achievements, has performed at the Grand Old Opry and other major Christian conventions.

and fractured lives. We go in the door with our assortment of broken things, but we leave with new, repaired, replaced, restored and fixed things!

The simple message of the song, along with the simple, down-home style of delivery reminds me to this day of the uncomplicated way that Jesus loves every one of us. How is it that we lose sight of these simple truths? How is it that we allow the Christian life to get so complicated at times, when at its heart it consists of the simple truth that Jesus is the Carpenter who waits for us to bring him broken things to mend?

The reference to Jesus as a Carpenter comes from the Gospel of Mark:

Jesus left there and went to his hometown, accompanied by his disciples. When the Sabbath came, he began to teach in the synagogue, and many who heard him were amazed.

"Where did this man get these things?" they asked. "What's this wisdom that has been given him, that he even does miracles! Isn't this the carpenter? Isn't this Mary's son and the brother of James, Joseph, Judas and Simon? Aren't his sisters here with us?" And they took offense at him.

Jesus said to them, "Only in his hometown, among his relatives and in his own house is a prophet without honor" (Mark 6:1-4).

Does anyone believe it was a total accident that Jesus became a carpenter while he was on earth? Personally, I think this unique reality speaks volumes about the nature of Christ the man, Christ the human, Christ the one who could relate to people—and Christ the one who could understand pain, what a broken heart felt like and how the world could inflict damage and injustice. Christ was a carpenter because it helped him keep his feet on the ground so to speak; it helped him stay connected with the people he came to save, the normal, everyday people—people like you and me.

As stated in the introduction, everyone has their own mental image of Jesus, what he looked like, how he would have acted and what he would be like if he suddenly appeared on earth again. I'm convinced that no matter what century he would have picked to become human, taking on the role of a carpenter would have been something universal and somehow non-threatening to anyone. I'm a person who believes that everything in scripture was included on purpose, as well as everything that wasn't included.

For some reason, we weren't supposed to know what Jesus looked like physically. Nor do we know much of anything about his childhood. But we were supposed to know what kind of work he did as an adult, prior to his ministry. If it was important enough to be included in the most important book ever written, it is worth pondering what was behind that decision—was there more to Jesus' earthly occupation than just another job until his real job started?

While I don't believe that any of the metaphors and images of Christ in scripture can be broken down into infinitely small particles, with unlimited meaning in each and every nuance, I do believe there will always be untapped richness in the Word of God, especially when it involves language describing our Savior, his work and his ministry—sometimes in his own words.

Matt. 13:5 says, "Isn't this the carpenter's son?" I also don't think it was a coincidence that Jesus followed in his earthly father's footsteps as a carpenter. There are two main things carpenters do: create things and fix things. When you consider the spiritual aspect of Jesus obeying his heavenly father as well, it kind of gives a new meaning to having a family business, doesn't it?

On one hand, we should never forget the simplicity of why Jesus became human, and what he offers to mankind. On the other hand, without extending metaphors to their breaking point, I think we would do well to take a closer look at the significance of his becoming a carpenter. Out of all the many occupations available, even in the first century, why did he choose that particular one? Is it possible there is more to Jesus' role as a carpenter than meets the eye? Is there more meaning and take-home value imbedded that we might not have considered before?

*"If thou desire the love of God and man, be humble;
for the proud heart, as it loves none but itself,
so it is beloved of none but itself."*
Francis Quarles (1592 – 1694)

Two

The Master Craftsman

Everyone has something that needs to be repaired. Compare, if you will, our inner selves—our attitudes, emotions, memories, desires—with our physical homes. Perhaps doing this will make it easier for some to relate to the special scriptural image of Christ the Carpenter. Similar to the many images of Christ that this series will explore, there are also many scriptures about the image of God, of which I have listed only a few. Some describe how we were created in the image of God; others about how we are being transformed back into God's image:

"So God created man in his own image, in the image of God he created him; male and female he created them" (Gen. 1:27).

"This is the written account of Adam's line. When God created man, he made him in the likeness of God" (Gen. 5:1).

"And have put on the new self, which is being renewed in knowledge in the image of its Creator" (Col. 3:10).

"And we, who with unveiled faces all reflect the Lord's glory, are being transformed into his likeness with ever-increasing glory, which comes from the Lord, who is the Spirit" (2 Cor. 3:18).

All homeowners know there is *always* something that needs to be fixed, replaced, repaired or upgraded in their homes. Actor Tim Allen became wildly popular with his very funny series, "Home Improvement." Why was the show such a phenomenal success? I believe it was because virtually every homeowner could relate to Tim's endless series of challenges and his often hilarious, creative solutions. What man doesn't want to make the lawnmower or garbage disposal more powerful so they work better, faster and more efficiently?

All homes, even new homes (ironically), need *something* sooner or later (usually sooner!). A room needs to be enlarged, a plumbing problem erupts, a squeaky door needs to be fixed, a storm window needs to be replaced or a new floor or new carpeting needs to be installed—it is literally a never ending list!

It is the same with *hearts* as with homes—something *always* needs attention, fixing, replacing or improving. There is never a time when everything is perfect. But to where do we go when our heart is *broken*? To whom do we turn when our spirit is *crushed*? Where do we take our heart when it *hurts*, when it needs some kind of special attention that isn't responding to our normal, usual efforts? What do we do when nothing we do seems to work—when what we really need is a heart professional? Unfortunately, this kind of problem isn't as easily solved as adding more voltage.

Do we turn to the Yellow Pages? The classified ads? The Internet? In today's world, it is possible to get just about anything repaired or replaced—for a price, of course. But something even the mildly rich have found out is there is just not enough money in the world to repair a damaged heart (much less for the "heart repairman" to make house calls). Oh sure, we can have the physical heart organ repaired, even replaced, but you know that's not the heart I'm talking about.

I'm talking about the invisible heart, the one that we try to fix (some call it medicate), or intoxicate, or deceive or distract—anything to dull the ache, to fill the void or cure whatever its problem is. But nothing seems to work, and sometimes we are simply desperate to do something, anything, to find peace, to experience happiness, to stumble across the magic formula that will calm it down and make the pain go away once and for all.

Countless millions have tried to fix their heart problem with alcohol—but has that ever worked? Isn't it always the opposite? How many homes and lives has alcohol ruined? Others try drugs…with the same or worse results. Pick your poison—what is your self-prescribed medication of choice? Sex, pornography, gambling, eating, crime, apathy? More importantly, have any of them ever worked? Having tried most of the above, I think I know the answer.

At this point, I want to sound like the TV ads, "But wait! Don't despair! There is a place! I know a guy!" The difference is this is for real, and although it's not available for $19.99 plus shipping and handling, it is quite the bargain, all things considered. What's the catch? What's the bottom line? In a nutshell, you give the Carpenter all your broken pieces and he gives you something priceless—a brand new heart. "Okay, now pick up that phone! Call NOW!"

I'm joking of course, but the truth is we really can take our heart to the Carpenter's Shop, regardless of how badly it is damaged. He's the master carpenter. No job is too big or too small, and all his work is guaranteed…eternally. In short, he's simply the best in the business. Actually, he stands alone in his business because he really can't be duplicated. No one else does the work he does.

The only problem is not everyone knows about this place. Not everyone knows about this Carpenter. But I do, and many others do as well. We found a place to take our broken hearts, our damaged, shredded, crushed and pain-filled hearts. Thank God there is a place! Thank God there is a guy! And unlike every one of our own prescriptions, which like Tim the Tool Man consistently fail, this is a solution that never fails. I'm sure if you ask around, someone you know also knows how to get hold of the Carpenter.

*"He who learns must suffer, and, even in our sleep,
pain that cannot forget falls drop by drop upon the
heart, and in our own despair, against our will,
comes wisdom to us by the awful grace of God."*
Aeschylus (525 – 456 BC)

Three

A Walking Ghetto

Let's take another look at the parallel between the human heart and our home or a building. This is not a new concept, and in fact several scriptures make use of it:

"Do you not know that your body is a temple of the Holy Spirit?" (1Cor. 6:19).

"In him the whole building is joined together and rises to become a holy temple in the Lord" (Eph. 2:21).

"You also, like living stones, are being built into a spiritual house to be a holy priesthood" (1Pet. 2:5).

Most everyone who knew me when I was growing up was shocked to see me after I left my small hometown in Wisconsin and returned a few years later—completely burned out on drugs and alcohol. Many who didn't know me then but who know me today as a healthy Christian, simply wouldn't have recognized me at all before Christ (and not just because of my beard and long hair).

My house needed *major* remodeling. My spirit needed *extensive* renovating. The truth was my entire structure needed bulldozing! Anyone who has seen the TV show, "Extreme Makeover," mentioned by Jeff Black in the Foreword, knows what is going to happen when the crew visits the problematic home featured in each episode. After sending the family off on a fabulous vacation, the first step is a simple one—level the house!

In August 1992, Hurricane Andrew hit south Florida with a fury, doing more damage than any previous storm in America's history. My wife and I were shocked as we drove by thousands of homes, so many damaged beyond repair. It was obvious that all anyone could do was to bring in a bulldozer, clear the site and start over. Half of south Florida needed an extreme makeover.

My heart resembled the footage taken after such natural disasters as tornados and hurricanes—it was nothing but a tangled, mangled pile of debris and wreckage. Just like the same neighborhoods once contained fine homes but suddenly are unrecognizable after a major disaster, so my heart once was in perfect condition, but those days were gone and I had a real mess on my hands. Was there any hope anywhere for me?

My life used to be that devastated. My heart had been exposed to a hurricane of sin and rebellion. My spiritual self looked like it had been hit by a tornado—all that was left was a twisted pile of useless rubble. While it is true that some of the damage came at the hands of my father during many long years of very serious physical and emotional abuse, it is also true that I added my own storm of self-destruction.

I had decided to make up for all of the years of Dad's cruelty, and I completely rebelled against everything I had ever been taught about right and wrong. I started with alcohol and quickly graduated to drugs, first marijuana, and then very quickly started doing hard drugs. It wasn't long before I would take anything anyone had, and it simply didn't matter how I got the money to get my daily fix—or what it was I was swallowing or smoking. I was going to party hardy until the cows came home and no one was going to stop me.

It wasn't long at all, only a couple of years actually, of such daily abuse of my body that the toll became very evident, even to me. I realized I was destroying myself but it was like I was being pulled by an alien tractor beam and was unable to change course. The day I took a long, hard look at my condition and firmly believed I would never be happy again was the day I decided enough was enough—22 years of living in misery was long enough. I decided to put an end to the pain and I took 350 sleeping pills.

It was only because a friend found me and called an ambulance that I did not die, but instead woke up in the Intensive Care Unit of a hospital—I had been unconscious for 48 hours. The doctor told me I was fortunate to be alive and that they had nearly lost me. I believed them. But as I lay there in the dark and quiet that night, I really started to panic. Now what? I couldn't try that again because I might fail again. Really, what was I going to do now? My desperation peaked, and I was literally at the lowest point of my entire life—and most of it was my own fault.

My house was rapidly nearing complete dilapidation, something I had never been more aware of than at that moment in the hospital. I had never felt more desperately in need of major reconstruction. I sensed the wrecking ball just around corner. The problem was there was no way to fix such extensive damage. I was positive it would be impossible. Who or what would even be capable, much less willing, to take on such a hopeless challenge? And especially for a nobody like me?

I was a walking ghetto of my former self. To think only a few short years before I had received a letter in the mail inviting me to the tryouts for the 1972 Olympics, and I almost certainly would have made the first U.S. gold medal archery team (it had been an exhibition sport until then). I knew this because the 3rd man on the team had been 3rd under me at nationals the year before. That tournament was my fondest memory, receiving a real gold medal at the U.S. Nationals in 1969, at 17 years of age, winning the men's division. This of course came about only because of four hours of practice every day after school and tournaments every weekend for the previous three years. But all that was gone now, completely gone, and never again would be part of my life. I doubted that day if I could have hit the broad side of a barn.

*"If you plan to build a tall house of virtues,
you must first lay deep foundations of humility."*
St. Augustine of Hippo (354 – 430)

Four

The Carpenter's Shop

Thank God, I finally went to the right place! Some people stopped me on the street one day and tried to tell me about it. Wherever I went, it seemed someone was trying to convince me about it. Finally, one day, someone had the courage to tell me—while I was arguing with them—that I was *blind*. Somehow, I knew it was true. Thank God, I finally listened and next thing I knew I had stumbled into the Carpenter's Shop!

I had passed by it countless times before in my life but never even considered entering. Actually, I had been to the shop quite often as kid—forced to go is more accurate—but never had been too much impressed. Oh sure, it was nice enough, and there were a few really nice people there but it just didn't mean that much to me at the time. I basically went there for baseball (and there was a girl in the youth group who I liked) and to get away from home for another couple of hours. No one had ever explained to me that the Carpenter had something to offer to me, personally.

Now things were very different. Now I was in a state of desperation, pouring out my heart, crying at the Carpenter's feet, begging him for help. I didn't know what to expect or if my cries would fall on deaf ears. Part of me thought I might just be making a big fool of myself. The other part of me was too desperate to care. All I knew was that if this didn't work, I honestly didn't have any other options. The thought crossed my mind, and I didn't rule it out, that I might even attempt again what I had failed to accomplish before.

A surprising thing happened. The Carpenter actually responded to my blubbering, incoherent prayer. He not only responded, but suddenly I knew he was real and that he had always been real—and not only that but I knew he *loved* me. In a single instant, I knew he had been patiently waiting for me, that he had been only a prayer away the entire time. He surrounded my entire being with the best sense of *peace* that I had ever experienced. My heart suddenly felt warm…and strangely content. Something I had not experienced in a very long time began to bubble up inside me and I realized with a start that it was *joy*. Those three words, love, peace and joy had become a joke to me. No one ever really found things like that. It was all a big rip off. Life had nothing good to offer. But I could not possibly have been more wrong. This was all real—this was beyond amazing!

Then an even stranger thing happened. The Carpenter said that he and I needed to sit down and have a long talk. The first thing we did was to stand together and survey the hopeless condition of my life and my spirit.

I felt an intense, burning shame. How had things gotten so bad, so quickly? Surely I could have managed some basic maintenance; surely I could have done *something* more than I had, which was basically nothing constructive. Now it was probably going to be condemned. It just seemed an impossible mess, and even this nice Carpenter probably had his limitations. At the same time, no one had ever touched my heart the way he did and, for the first time in many years,

I had a surge of hope that somehow things were going to be okay. Finally, I believed I had found the answer.

The Carpenter had a very unexpected response. He asked, "Do you trust me?"

"Yeah, I guess so," I said, a little unsure of where this was going. Then we had the following conversation:

"Son, you're going to have to sign over the title to your house and property, and you'll have to give me the keys. You're going to have to let go of it completely."

"What do you mean, let go? That's why I'm here, so you can help me. What's to hang on to?"

"I can't help you if you won't let go."

"Why wouldn't I? Look around, this place is a disaster, and I would give anything to have it restored. It used to be quite a handsome house, you know."

"Yes, I do know. And it can be beautiful again—even better than before. But are you willing to turn all of it over to my care, and not just the parts that are the worst off?"

"Sure, I guess so, who wouldn't?"

"Believe me, I've known many before you who could only give me half, or maybe most, but chose to keep the rest to work on themselves."

"But that's crazy! Why come to you and then only allow you to partially repair things? Why would I want to live in a place that's only part or most of the way fixed?"

"You'll see, son, and then you'll understand."

"God has two dwellings: one in heaven,
and the other in a meek and thankful heart."
Izaak Walton (1593 – 1683)

Five

The Carpenter's Toolbox

I did come to understand, eventually. It took awhile, mostly because I discovered that I had a whole lot of mistrust in my heart. And just as the Carpenter had known, I didn't let him into all the parts of my house, at least not right away. As a matter of fact, sometimes I actually ran him off, just when things were starting take shape—even though it didn't make any sense whatsoever. It was just some kind of instinct or reflex that kept reacting, like a frog leg that kicks even after the frog is dead. I was even amazed myself sometimes that I just couldn't bring myself to a place of total trust—no matter how much good the Carpenter did for me and no matter that I had no real reason whatsoever not to trust him. Was this proof that I was beyond help, beyond fixing?

Then, invariably, I'd call him back again, begging him not to abandon me, apologizing profusely. Again and again this happened, even after the Carpenter had done extensive work on my foundation, even after he had installed all new joists, walls and trusses—still I found that I couldn't bring myself to a position of complete and total trust. It was exactly as he had predicted. It was like he knew me better than I knew myself.

One of the sad things following hurricane Andrew was that homeowners experienced a wave of rip-off artists who blended in with real contractors coming from all over the country to help rebuild. Most contractors came to do honest work and to earn honest money. A few evil ones took huge deposits from insurance checks and never came back to do the work. Because of a few bad apples, suddenly all contractors were criminals and none could be trusted. A major wave of panic enveloped south Florida, which turned into a firestorm of hostility and mistrust. Suddenly even well established, honest and proven contractors were held in suspicion.

Very similar to the ripped-off homeowners of Miami, in my youth I had an extremely hard time trusting anyone, which automatically transferred to my relationship with my new heart contractor. It took a very long time for the Carpenter to convince me that my job was a personal project for him; that he was not only capable of doing the work but that he was the original builder of my house. He knew every nail and screw, every board, pipe and shingle. On top of that, it seemed very important to the Carpenter that I learn to trust him. So I began to make a concerted effort. After all, who else had ever cared that much or had done so much for me?

One of my all-time favorite hymns is, "What a Friend We Have In Jesus." The lyrics are very familiar to most people:

What a friend we have in Jesus,
all our sins and griefs to bear;
What a privilege to carry
everything to Him in prayer.

Why is it that we can't, in reality, carry *anything* and *everything* to the Carpenter without reservation? Why is it that we can't seem to give him the keys and the title to our heart's home; our inner self, our soul? What stops us just short of total commitment, or *absolute* surrender as writer, pastor and evangelist Andrew Murray worded it? Was it as simple as pride or was it something else?

After 35 years with the Carpenter—who is still working on my house to this day—I believe I may have recently found an answer to the question. I believe we hold back for the very same reason we hesitated to go to the Carpenter's Shop in the first place.

Oh, we knew the Carpenter was there, no matter what we said to impress our friends about how tough or cool we were. Everyone knew the stories, or knew someone who had their heart fixed. Some were truly amazing stories, and some of those people had gone on to do incredible things. But like most, it really wasn't such a mystery why we held back. We simply feared the unknown. We mistrusted even this good and honest Carpenter because of age-old, simple *fear*. The painful truth is that we never really get rid of all that fear. Some of it will continue to plague us throughout our Christian life.

Have you ever watched hospital scenes in Civil War movies? It's pretty scary stuff. The exhausted and overworked doctors basically arrived with a needle and thread, a hammer, a saw and a bottle of whiskey—perhaps a piece of wood to hold between your teeth. So it was at first with the Carpenter, and the fearsome looking box of tools he brought to my doorstep. What if that saw slipped? What if he hammered too hard, drilled too deep or shaved away too much? What if? What if?

I didn't have much trouble bringing small things for him to fix—maybe a new screen door or a rain gutter—but when he said I needed a whole new roof system, and all new wiring and plumbing, that was something else entirely.

When he said all the old had to come out so he could put in everything new, that was just a little too scary at the time.

In time, ever so gradually, I learned the Carpenter wasn't an ordinary contractor. Not only did he know every intimate detail of my heart but he also knew just how to fix everything. He never cut too much. He never drilled too deep. In fact, he never made a single mistake. I never heard him say, "Darn, I cut it twice, and it's still too short!" I never heard him say, "OOPS! Sorry about that!"

Eventually, I learned that even though the Carpenter never used modern power tools, the specialized type of carpentry he did superseded the ability of any of the tools he once held in his hands. The Carpenter's heart tools are timeless—he never needs new or better tools; he never needs to make trips to Home Depot. Human hearts are still the same, as they always have been and always will be.

I have tried to envision the Carpenter from Nazareth working when he was on the earth—and the tools of the time that he had at his disposal. What would have been in his toolbox? Probably a couple of different manual cross-cut saws, probably some hand-drills with various bits, surely a crude mallet or two, some chisels and so on.

In my mind's eye, I saw him thinking often about the rich parallels with his coming ministry as he shaped and fitted together the various parts of a supporting structure. Even though he was working with wood, I imagined how he would mostly be thinking about the various parts of a family, or a body of believers, and how he would be busy fitting and joining them together. I could see him in my mind's eye sawing off branches and knots, all the while envisioning the beautiful finished masterpiece. He would also foresee resistance to the saw as he encountered a particularly hard or knotted area of the wood. He would just proceed that much more carefully when working with such areas, knowing the ultimate beauty and usefulness that was at stake.

As he sawed, planed and smoothed, I imagined him thinking about the infinite number of rough edges on the collective human race with whom he soon would be working in a very similar way. After completing the sanding process, I envisioned the Carpenter getting out his finishing materials, rubbing in oils to bring out the rich, natural beauty of the wood.

He must have smiled to himself as he foresaw so many smooth, lustrous, finished works that he had worked from start to finish. Each of the various pieces had started the same, as a rough log or branch—some surely that had been discarded by others as twisted and useless—but now the whole world could see the full extent of the beauty, which had been inherent within them all along, but just needed the hands of a master craftsman to reveal it. As he surveyed each finished piece, each unique work of art, it must have occurred to him that even the imperfections, even those difficult areas, had become beautiful parts of the whole, giving each piece its own distinct character, charm and unique beauty.

Going far beyond the physical abilities of the tools at his disposal, I came to understand that this Carpenter also has the gifted sight of an artist. He has much more in mind than function and practicality. I was to learn that the greatest desire of his heart was to create works of timeless beauty and inspiration—over and over again, never tiring in the least of producing masterpieces, no matter how long each one took, how much effort or how much sacrifice.

In this sense, he was very much like the great artist and sculptor, Michelangelo, who envisioned finished figures trapped in huge blocks of marble, needing only to be set free. The Carpenter had an even more uncanny ability to foresee incredible, finished beauty locked in every rough log and cracked, warped slab of timber that came into his shop.

It was a precious thought to realize he always asked permission of his subjects to work on them before getting out his tools and starting the process of setting them free.

*"He Himself bore our sins in His body on the cross,
so that we might die to sin and live to righteousness;
for by His wounds you were healed."*
1 Peter 2:24

Six

The Original Innocence Project

One day, I asked the Carpenter about the source of his incredible abilities. There seemed to be literally nothing he couldn't do. He told me something that I didn't fully understand at the time but eventually did. He said, "I had to be broken first—it's the secret of my power." To be honest, I had heard the story before (when I was a kid) about how he had been broken, but somehow had managed to dismiss it as very tragic, yet not something that affected my life one way or the other. When the Carpenter told me the story personally, however, suddenly it took on a whole new meaning and personal significance.

Without going into too many gory details, he basically explained how he had been betrayed by a friend, arrested by the authorities and taken in the middle of the night before a judge—even though that was not legal in that part of the world at the time. When the judge couldn't find anything wrong with him, he passed the buck to the governor, who also deep down knew the man was not guilty of anything. Not having the courage to do the right thing, he decided to protect his job instead and let a mob decide the Carpenter's fate. This turned into the definition of a disgraceful public spectacle and the ultimate mockery of justice.

A current movement in the offices of district attorneys around the country is called the Innocence Project.[3] For dozens of inmates who were wrongly convicted before DNA evidence existed, this movement comes on the wings of angels. Some who have been incarcerated for 10, 15 and 20 years or more are being released when DNA analysis finally proves them innocent. As of this writing, 244 inmates around the country have been exonerated—including 17 death row inmates, and one who had been in prison for 23 years. It is hard to imagine the mixed feelings in the hearts of those falsely convicted inmates upon hearing the good news of their release.

In the case of the Carpenter though, there was no such thing as an Innocence Project coming to his rescue. The futile voices of protest against the massive injustice were drowned out by the bloodthirsty mob. To make a long and painful story short, they gave the Carpenter the death penalty for his non-existent crimes. Ironically, the man whose craft was working with wood ended up being nailed to a wooden crossbeam.

As the Carpenter described this to me, while I followed the story in his book describing the events, I began to understand that he first had to be broken in order to be able to mend others. I also began to understand for the first time the real meaning of breaking bread during the Lord's Table. *"Take and eat of my brokenness,"* he said, *"Take and eat of my body, the bread of life; take and drink of my lifeblood, the wine of forgiveness"* (Matt. 26:26, paraphrased). He really does understand all about our brokenness!

Wasn't it true that when the early believers came together to fellowship, they called it "breaking bread" (Acts 2:42-46)? So when the Carpenter broke bread with me, or had

---

[3] The Innocence Project home page: http://www.innocenceproject.org.

fellowship with me in my heart, it was only possible because he himself had been broken, and had thus made the way for me to "break bread" with him.

Tears welled up in my eyes the first time I heard these words with my heart and "knew in my knower" that they were the truth. He had to suffer so others wouldn't have to suffer. His body was broken so others could eat the bread of life. Even though he was completely innocent, he had given himself so the guilty could be set free. In a sense, this made him the original innocence project—but inverted—in that he voluntarily took the punishment for the guilty, and then let them out of prison even though they didn't deserve it.

It was almost more than I could absorb when I envisioned all the horrible, bloody details involved in his torture and eventual death…because I couldn't stop thinking about his innocence, and how he could have stopped it at any time—but followed through to the bitter end because he cared that much…about guilty people like me. But the most amazing part by far was how his father in heaven brought him back to life—giving the breath of life back to his son, the Carpenter, and then speaking words that still echo around the world: "Believe these words and you will see they are true. Bring your broken things to the Carpenter and he will make them whole. Don't wait until tomorrow; he's waiting right now for you to bring to him your broken hearts, your broken lives, your broken marriages and families, your broken churches and communities…believe these words and you will see they are true…believe these words and you will be made new again!"

Go ahead and try; give him an opportunity. What I'm telling you is that if he could put someone like me back together—a real life Humpty Dumpty—I don't believe there is anything you can bring to him that he can't handle. I challenge you to give him a chance!

"It is easier to build a boy than to mend a man."
Author Unknown

Seven

Much More Than a Carpenter

The main premise of this book is not a new concept. In 2002, a heartwarming movie came out titled "Joshua." The main character, played by Tony Goldwyn, beautifully captured the metaphor of a mysterious carpenter who came to repair more than a dilapidated, neglected church building. Instead, he came to repair individuals, families and a community. A famous line is, "Sometimes you have to tear something down in order to build it back up."

Josh McDowell wrote a short book titled *More Than a Carpenter,* of which more than ten million copies are circulating around the world in multiple languages, and for good reason. At one point early in his very promising career as an academic, Josh said about Christianity, "That's for unthinking weaklings, not intellectuals." He called religion garbage and said Christians were "out of their minds." The book became a runaway bestseller because of Josh's determined journey to disprove Christianity, and his surprising discovery that he had been completely wrong. The village carpenter named Jesus had not been making crazy claims about being God but had simply spoken the truth. He really was more than a Carpenter—*much* more!

The image of Jesus the Carpenter is perhaps the most endearing of all his many images in scripture. He truly is the Lord Carpenter of our souls. No one understands us so well. No one else is capable or worthy of our utmost confidence and trust.

Let us remember the childlike simplicity with which each of us began our experience with the Carpenter. Let us remember the evangelist's simple song: *"He waits for us to bring him broken things to mend."* Let us not wait any longer. Let us come to him with our leaky roofs and damaged windows, our squeaky stairs and sagging floors, our wobbly chairs and falling apart drawers and yes, even our stiff wooden necks. May we realize afresh that we can trust the Carpenter with even the most twisted, knot-filled heart, with even the most cracked, dried out, warped soul; that he welcomes all into his Shop and turns no job down.

Let us submit to his cutting, drilling and hammering; his planing, shaving and sanding—knowing that when he's finished, we'll emerge from the pile of curled shavings and sawdust a magnificent new creation, totally remade in the image and vision of Christ the Master Carpenter. Each of us will come alive again, like a real life Pinocchio, ready to live a brand new life, ready to fulfill our purpose for existing.

Go ahead and give the Carpenter a call. His shop is always open—24/7/365. There is always a shop nearby, but if you can't find one, the Carpenter has assistants all over the world ready to point you in the right direction. The Carpenter's Shop is a place where anything can be fixed, but you'll have to remember his rules. You will have to give him the keys to your home—your heart, your soul. Like a slab of wood heading for its first encounter with a saw blade, you will have to yield to him completely. You will have to trust him implicitly. He simply won't have it any other way.

Once you've experienced his workmanship, however, you won't call anyone else—you won't need to!

*"Some want to live within the
sound of church or chapel bell.
I want to run a rescue shop
within a yard of hell."*
C. T. Studd (1860 – 1931)

Eight
Today is the Day!

There are many reasons to put off your personal encounter with the Carpenter, or your personal "moment of truth" as I like to describe it, but if you are honest you will admit that not a single one of them is a good reason. The Bible says in Hebrews 4:7, *"Today if you hear his voice, do not harden your hearts."*

The Romans Road[4]
Have you ever taken a trip down the Roman's Road? Did you know that you are literally only seven steps away from entering the Carpenter's Shop?
- **Step 1**: Realize that no one is good enough, nor can they make themselves good enough, to get into heaven on their own merits. Romans 3:10 says, *"As it is written: 'There is no one righteous, not even one.'"*
- **Step 2**: Confess the truth that you are a sinner. Romans 3:23 says, *"All have sinned and fall short of the glory of God."*

---

[4] See more details at http://www.allaboutgod.com/the-roman-road.htm.

- **Step 3**: Recognize where sin came from. Romans 5:12 says, *"Therefore, just as sin entered the world through one man, and death through sin, and in this way death came to all men, because all sinned."*
- **Step 4**: Acknowledge that God has placed a terrible price on sin. Romans 6:23 says, *"The wages of sin is death, but the gift of God is eternal life in Christ Jesus our Lord."*
- **Step 5**: Believe that Christ died for the sins of the world, which includes your sins. Romans 5:8 says, *"But God demonstrates his own love for us in this: While we were still sinners, Christ died for us."*
- **Step 6**: Take God at His word. Romans 10:13 says, *"Everyone who calls on the name of the Lord will be saved."*
- **Step 7**: Claim God's promises for your salvation. Romans 10:9-11 says, *"If you confess with your mouth, 'Jesus is Lord,' and believe in your heart that God raised him from the dead, you will be saved. For it is with your heart that you believe and are justified, and it is with your mouth that you confess and are saved. As the Scripture says, 'Anyone who trusts in him will never be put to shame.'"*

Now that you have taken these seven steps, you are seconds away from the salvation of your soul. I'm providing a sample prayer for you to pray, but feel free to use your own words. Prayer is simply conversing with God. He is not impressed with fancy words or something you found in a book.

Whenever I pray with inmates after a chapel service, I usually ask all of them to pray the prayer out loud. That way, no one will feel self-conscious. Before all the inmates begin to pray together, I tell them, "The only thing that matters, the only thing that impresses the Carpenter is that you are sincere. You're the only one in the world who knows whether or not you mean it when you pray this prayer. But you can be assured that if you are sincere, he will know—he won't miss it, and he will respond to your prayer."

Following this salvation prayer is a prayer of gratitude for the Carpenter who came to earth to set an example for how to live the perfect life on earth, and then sacrificed himself for the sins of mankind. Because of his sacrifice, we can experience fellowship with him while on earth and then glorious eternity with him in heaven.

Salvation Prayer[5]

God, I recognize that I have not lived my life for You up until now. I have been living for myself and that is wrong. I need You in my life; I want You in my life. I acknowledge the completed work of Your Son Jesus Christ in giving His life for me on the cross at Calvary, and I long to receive the forgiveness you have made freely available to me through this sacrifice. Come into my life now, Lord. Take up residence in my heart and be my king, my Lord and my Savior. From this day forward, I will no longer be controlled by sin, or the desire to please myself, but I will follow You all the days of my life. Those days are in Your hands. I ask this in Jesus' precious and holy name. Amen.

---

[5] From http://www.allaboutgod.com/salvation-prayer.htm.

A Prayer of Gratitude to the Carpenter

Lord Jesus, You have given us so much, and have done so much for us. It hardly seems possible that you would consider all of that only a beginning. Yet, You have much more to give us, and You have so much more to do for us. All we have to do is come to You, and turn over to Your care the things in our lives that need to be repaired and made new.

We are so very grateful that we have such a loving, caring Carpenter to whom we can come, anytime, anywhere and bring anything. We humble ourselves before You and we ask You to mend our hearts, restore them by Your touch, and we will overflow with thankfulness. Help us Lord to learn to put everything, our entire lives, in Your hands.

In Jesus' name. Amen.

ABOUT THE AUTHOR

Kevin Hrebik grew up with his two brothers, Kris and Karl, in a suburb of Chicago. His parents, Bill and Louise, temporarily separated when Kevin was in 6th grade, and the family moved to rural Wisconsin. From Kevin's earliest memories, his Dad always had been extremely abusive, but things got a lot worse during the six months his Mom was gone. Even when she returned, nothing seemed capable of stemming his father's violence or his excessive drinking. He vented his rage on the entire family on a daily basis, often using very creative methods to inflict the maximum pain. Years later, two more brothers came along, Kurt and Kenny, but Bill died while Louise was pregnant with Kenny. Thankfully, neither of his last two sons would experience their father's abuse.

Shortly after graduating from high school, after breaking the law, getting arrested, and sitting in jail for 11 days, Kevin was given two years probation and released. He left home at age 18, and promptly dove headfirst into drug and alcohol abuse. Within a few years, he got in trouble with the law again, and spent 101 days in jail when he couldn't post a mere $100 bail.

Kevin became a Christian in 1974 while living in a drug rehab ministry in Wisconsin called New Life, and shortly after that joined Jesus People USA, a live-in ministry in Chicago, where he stayed for the next five years. While in Chicago, he wrote for their ministry magazine, *Cornerstone*, which began to be distributed in prisons nationwide, and Kevin took on the job of responding to prisoners who wrote to *Cornerstone.*

Upon leaving the ministry in 1980, he pursued freelance writing, and since then has nearly 30 years of experience in many aspects of the writing and publishing world. He began writing poetry and fiction, and for many years wrote greeting cards and product texts for multiple publishers. He has written high school and adult Sunday school curriculum, as well as numerous newspaper and magazine articles. He has been an assignment writer for *Charisma* magazine, and copyeditor for the publisher of the world-famous "Chicken Soup for the Soul" series.

Kevin has an AS in Journalism, a BA in Interpersonal Communication, and a MA in Religion. As of this writing, he is a Doctor of Ministry student at Houston Graduate School of Theology, and serves as a Chaplain at the Harris County Jail, the 3rd largest jail system in the nation. He and his wife, Cara, attend Hope Community Evangelical Covenant Church in Houston. Kevin is licensed by the ECC denomination as a bi-vocational minister.

All proceeds from this book, and speaking engagements to promote the book, will go toward Kevin's support as a home missionary chaplain to jails and prisons. For more information about this book, Kevin's jail ministry, or to schedule him to speak at your church, contact him at hopebehindbars@sbcglobal.net. You may also be interested in receiving the free, monthly E-newsletter of Hope Behind Bars.

REVIEWS

"This simple, yet poignant story about the Carpenter allows each to determine his or her own brokenness and then to rejoice in knowing where to go for mending. In this world of expensive, exotic and well-advertised cures, how welcome is a sweet home remedy. Looking at the pain on faces encountered during the day, on all walks and byways, cellblocks, halfway houses, highways and malls, the power of the message of *The Carpenter's Shop* stands out as an answer to a prayer asked or not even asked, yet. Placing this small book into the hands of those seeking, searching, or just writhing, calls out for them as they strive for the voice to say it themselves, *'Save me, O my God'* (Psalm 3:7). What a blessing to rejoice in brokenness as a path to Him."

Lina Liken-Paske, Ed.D., CAP
Delray Beach, FL

"The author of this book is my brother, and is a pretty good carpenter himself. He speaks from the voice of experience of hands and heart. As a carpenter and former builder myself, I can attest to Kevin's words that no house is perfect and every house new or old needs some work. In this book, Kevin vividly weaves the imagery of the earthly house and our spiritual house. When your earthly house is completely broken down, you are likely to seek a professional craftsman to do the work. But too often we think our house only needs a little fixing up, and we try to do the work ourselves. And so it is with our spiritual house. As a pastor, I have often witnessed men's futile and failed attempts at 'do-it-yourself' repairs and rebuilding of their lives and spiritual homes. I have also seen the absolute joy and peace that comes upon those who turn the work over to the Master, and whose lives are completely transformed and made new by the Master Carpenter, Jesus. My brother Kevin is one of those so transformed, and this book that he has written will help many others to know and trust the only Master Carpenter who can do the same for all who believe in Him. If you don't know Him yet, let this book guide you to his shop. If you know Him as Lord and Savior, please pass this book on to one of the broken ones who so desperately needs to meet the Master Carpenter, Jesus Christ."

Karl Hrebik
Pastor, Crooked Run Baptist Church
Rapidan, VA

"Trials and tribulation are the foundation of all our stories. Each of us has a story that holds special meaning to only ourselves, unless it is shared with others. This short story is one that should open the door for the reader about the importance of allowing others into the rebuilding of our life and the effect we can have on others. God through the Holy Spirit is able to reconstruct us and to return us to Himself—like a broken vessel reassembled back to our original state. This story is about Grace and how God loves us so much, that even when we reject Him, He has not forgotten His covenant that He promised us. When we feel that we cannot be rebuilt, but that we will forever remain in sin and out of Grace, God performs another of what we call miracles. This book is a must for those who are yet to understand what it means to be Born Again."

Charles Frederick Tolbert, M.Div., M.Ed.
Pastor, Christ Found All Creation Saved
Boynton Beach, FL

"*The Carpenter's Shop* presents a powerful image of Christ as the master craftsman building and mending our broken lives. I believe Kevin Hrebik has captured the heart of Jesus in this brief story and the simple truths presented will ring true with all of us in our humanness."

Tye Riter
Pastor, Calvary Chapel West Boca
Boca Raton, FL

FEEDBACK

Did you enjoy this book?
Send your comments to Lisa@HaloPublishing.com.
Visit Halo's website at www.HaloPublishing.com.

COMING SOON

Watch for the next book in the
Images of Christ
series to be released soon:
Ten Clay Soldiers: Lessons from the Master Potter

LaVergne, TN USA
25 April 2010
180440LV00002B/1/P